P9-BYL-705

'Tis The Season To Be Crabby

by
SCHULZ

CollinsPublishersSanFrancisco
A Division of HarperCollins*Publishers*

Yuletide Blues

Christmas
Cards And
Letters

 **Christmas Cards And Letters**

Santa
Strikes
Again!

SANTA CLAUS IS DOWN AT THE CORNER..I HAVE A FEW QUESTIONS TO ASK HIM..

SO, MR. FANCY CLAUS, REMEMBER ME? MY NAME IS RERUN...

WHAT HAPPENED TO ALL THE THINGS YOU WERE GOING TO BRING ME FOR CHRISTMAS LAST YEAR? KIND OF FORGOT, DIDN'T YOU? HUH?!

You Don't
Always Get What
You Want

*Thank you again.
Happy New Year.
love, Sally*

A Packaged Goods Incorporated Book
First published 1996 by Collins Publishers San Francisco
1160 Battery Street, San Francisco, CA 94111-1213
http://www.harpercollins.com
Conceived and produced by Packaged Goods Incorporated
276 Fifth Avenue, New York, NY 10001
A Quarto Company

Copyright ©1996 United Feature Syndicate, Inc. All rights reserved.
HarperCollins ®, ☰®, and CollinsPublishersSanFrancisco™ are trademarks of
HarperCollins Publishers Inc.
PEANUTS is a registered trademark of United Feature Syndicate, Inc.
PEANUTS © United Feature Syndicate, Inc.

Based on the PEANUTS ® comic strip by Charles M. Schulz
http://www.unitedmedia.com
Library of Congress Cataloging-in-Publication Data
Schulz, Charles M.
[Peanuts. Selections]
'Tis the season to be crabby / by Schulz.
p.   cm.
ISBN 0-00-225218-X
I. Title
PN6728.P4S327   1996
741.5'973—dc20   96-17657
CIP

Printed in Hong Kong

1 3 5 7 9 10 8 6 4 2

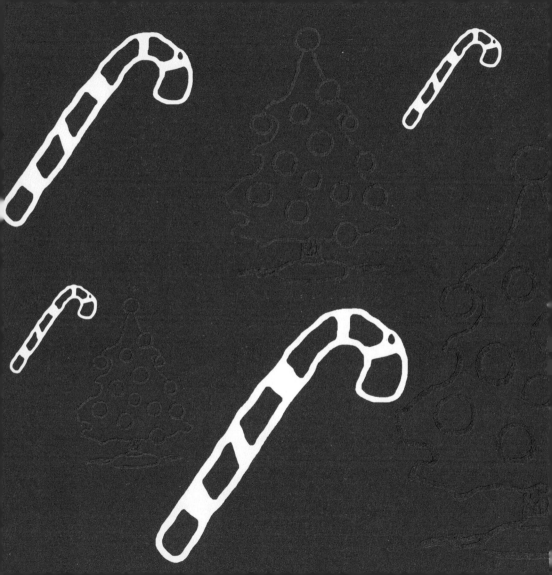

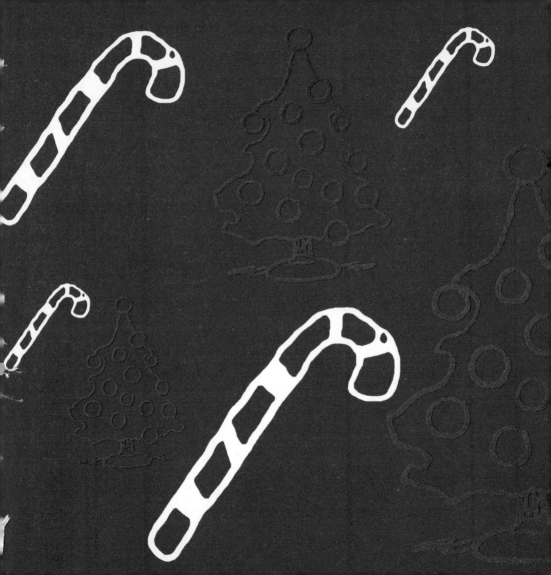